A Study in

Sherlockian

Aesthetic Realism:

Sherlock Holmes Cartoons

from a warped mind

Volume 1

By

Don Hobbs

Paperback ISBN 978-1-78705-860-6

Published by MX Publishing
335 Princess Park Manor, Royal Drive,
London, N11 3GX
www.mxpublishing.co.uk

Cover design by Brian Belanger

To

Joyce Hobbs, my lovely wife who has put up with my craziness for all these years.

Contents

221 Sherlockian Aesthetic Realism drawings by Don Hobbs with a canonical explanation accompanying each.

Foreword

This all started in the fall of 2011 when my wife Joyce and I stumbled across the Napoleon Museum during our "Roaming Rome" vacation. Inside there was an art exhibit by Chiam Koppleman, the American artist known for his works of Aesthetic Realism. The exhibit was entitled 'Napoleon Enters New York' and it featured drawings and paintings of Napoleon in various unfamiliar settings, like entering Coney Island or riding alligators. His Bicones hat and his epaulette-coat were always present in the pictures and something about this exhibit struck a chord with me. Immediately I knew I had to start my own series of drawings. Thus was born Aesthetic Sherlockian Realism. The pipe and deerstalker replace the epaulettes and Bicones. The Master replaces the Emperor. So enjoy my artistic adventure where the game is afoot.

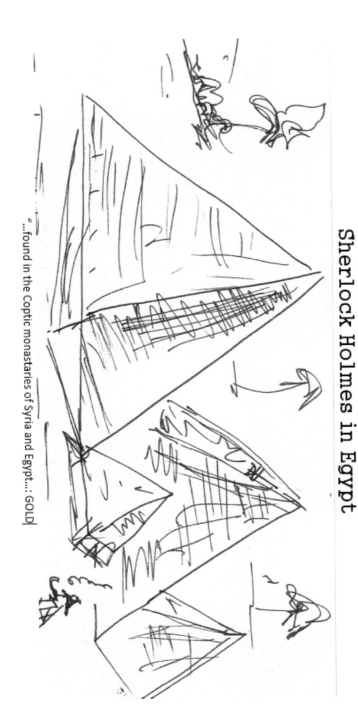

"...found in the Coptic monastaries of Syria and Egypt...: GOLD|

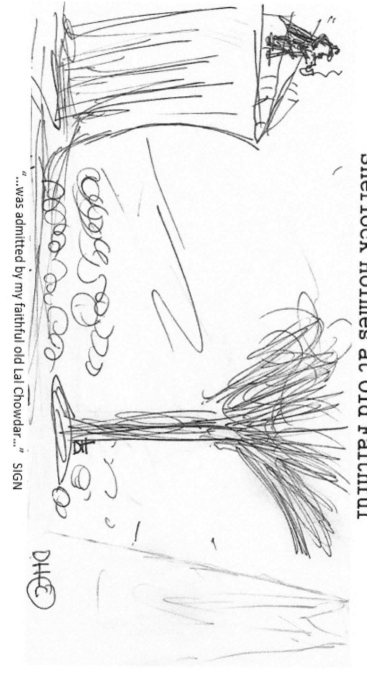

Sherlock Holmes at Old Faithful

"...was admitted by my faithful old Lal Chowdar..." SIGN

Sherlock Holmes at the Gum Ball Machine

10-30-11

"...just above the gum, the letter K three times repeated..." FIVE

"...A huge driving wheel and shaft, half filled with rubbish..." HOUN

DH 10·30·4

Sherlock Holmes Smoking in a Pumpkin Patch

"...so you can put that in your pipe and smoke it, Mr. Busybody Holmes..." SOLI

Sherlock Holmes Flies First Class

"...My dear Watson, First Class tickets and all expenses paid ..." Lady

10.30.11

11

Sherlock Holmes on the Moon

"...Possibly you are thinking of the connection between insanity and the phases of the moon ..." CREE

Sherlock Holmes Enjoys a Bath

"...Both Holmes and I had a weakness for the Turkish bath ..." ILLU

Sherlock Holmes Kicks a Field Goal

"...We advance, but the goal is afar ..." BRUC

Sherlock Holmes Enjoys a Frapuccino to Go

"...I sat with my coffee-cup halfway to my lips and stared at Barrymore..." HOUN

Sherlock Holmes at the Golden–Gate Bridge

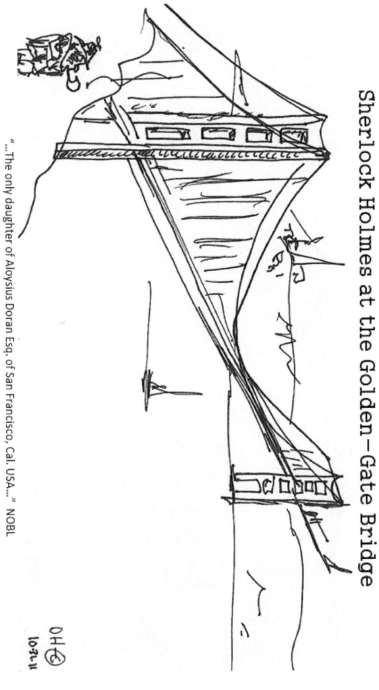

"...The only daughter of Aloysius Doran Esq. of San Francisco, Cal. USA..." NOBL

DH
10-31-11

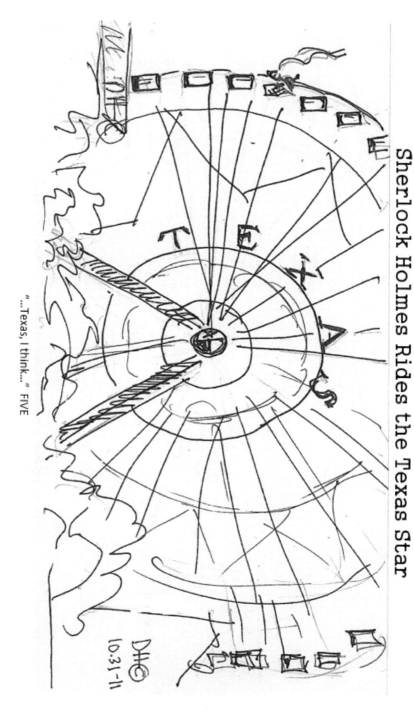

"...Texas, I think..." FIVE

"...proceeding in twos or threes along the sidewalk so as not to provoke attention..." VALL

Sherlock Holmes Rides an Elephant

"...then he was hit from a bullit from an elephant gun..." BLAN

Sherlock Holmes Rides a Harley–Davidson

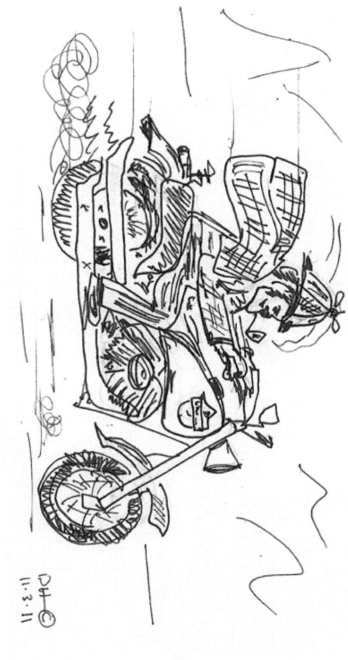

"...this is Baker Street not Harley Street..." SHOS

"...he had the entrée of every nightclub, doss house, and gambling-den in town...." ILLU

Sherlock Holmes Uses a Netty Pot

" "...in a nasal voice; "He grindeth slowly but exceeding small..." " ILLU

Sherlock Holmes Meets T–Rex

"...He had made his name as the most lewd and blood thirsty tyrant..." WIST

"...My way ran down a dried-up water course...." CROO

24

"...Well, then we must make a cross-country journey..." FINA

"...and the doctor has a prescription containing hot water and a lemon..." GOLD

Sherlock Holmes Listens to Sarasate on an iPod

"...Sarasate plays at St. James this afternoon ..." REDH

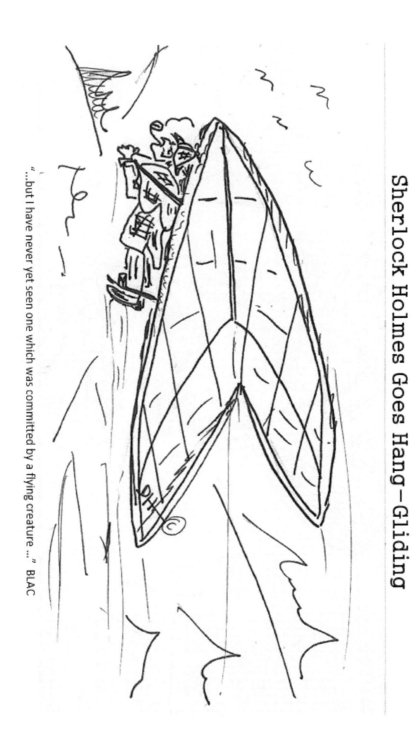

"...but I have never yet seen one which was committed by a flying creature ..." BLAC

"...Photography is one of my hobbies, he said ... " COPP

"...This way! This way! They are in the bowling-alley," he cried ...." SOLI

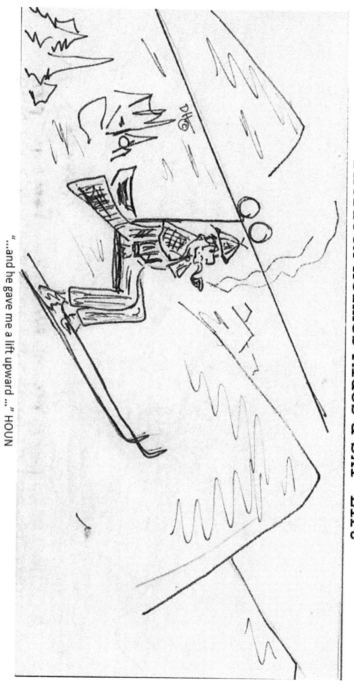

Sherlock Holmes Rides a Ski-Lift

"…and he gave me a lift upward …" HOUN

Sherlock Holmes Rides a Camel in the Daylight

" ...Sahara King was its name..."   VEIL

Sherlock Holmes Rides a Camel at Night

"...You see me now with a back like a camel ..." CROO

Sherlock Holmes Plays Polo

"...you play polo, you match them in every game ..." LAST

Sherlock Holmes in an X-34 Land Speeder

"...If we could fly out of that window hand in hand, hover over this great city ..." IDEN

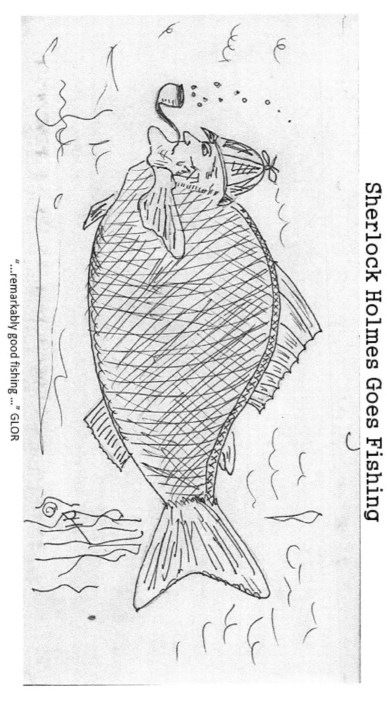

"...remarkably good fishing ... " GLOR

"...is so, it is a serious case. Nothing less would bring a man on such a day and at such an hour ..." FIVE

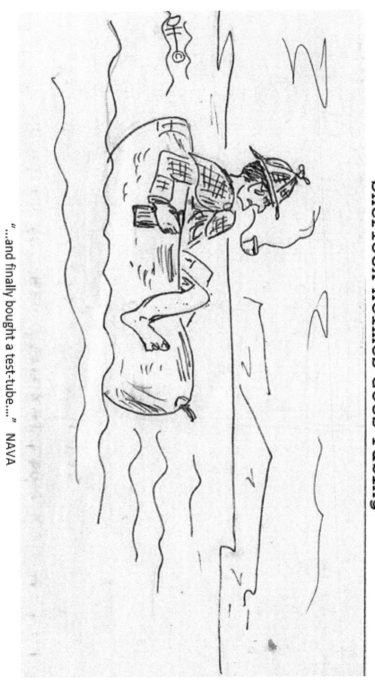

Sherlock Holmes Goes Tubing

" ...and finally bought a test-tube...." NAVA

Sherlock Holmes Wins the Heisman Trophy

"...It is to him that the trophy belongs..." BLUE

Sherlock Holmes at Cirque du Soleil – Quidam

"...with long bounds the huge black creature was leaping down the track..." HOUN

"...Here you are in your house, and me still picking my salt meat out of the harness cask..." GLOR

Sherlock Holmes Fixes a Toilet

"...he came into the room just as I finished my toilet..." 3STU

Sherlock Holmes Listens to Music

"...A loud thudding noise came from somewhere downstairs...." COPP

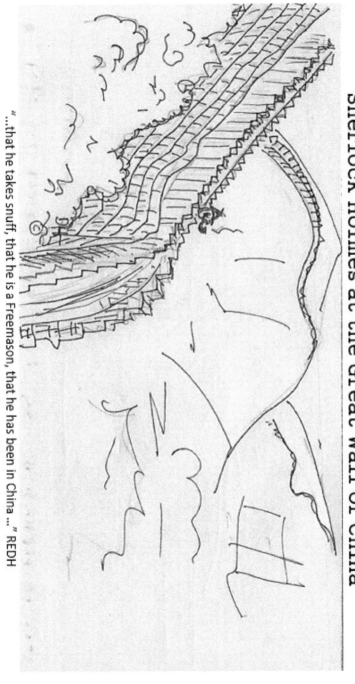

Sherlock Holmes at the Great Wall of China

"...that he takes snuff, that he is a Freemason, that he has been in China ..." REDH

Sherlock Holmes Goes to the Circus

" ...They are waiting for me at the cañon. Good-bye, my own darling -- good-bye...."   STUD

45

Sherlock Holmes in a Canoe

"...Tonga -- for that was his name -- was a fine boatman, and owned a big, roomy canoe of his own...." SIGN

46

Sherlock Holmes Checks the Weather

"...You like the weather?..." CHAS

47

Sherlock Holmes Makes a Wish

"...pushed down the board, rearranged the carpet, blew out the candles and walked straight into my arms..." NAVA

Sherlock Holmes Celebrates Christmas

"...Julia went there at Christmas two years ago..." SPEC

Sherlock Holmes Smiley Face

"...Holmes rose with a smile..." SECO

50

Sherlock Holmes Rides a Vespa

"...You see he poses as a motor expert and I keep a full garage..." LAST

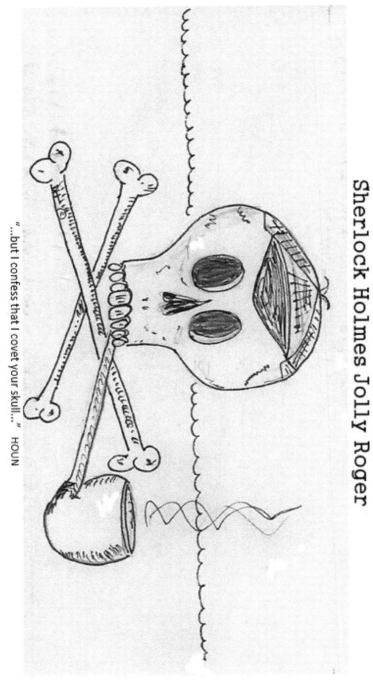

Sherlock Holmes Jolly Roger

"...but I confess that I covet your skull..." HOUN

52

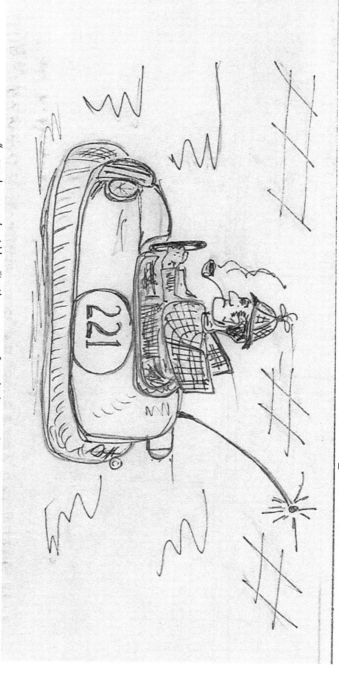

"...one bumper,' said he, "to the success of our little expedition...." SIGN

Sherlock Holmes and Watson Play Jeopardy

"...Come Watson, come!" he cried. "The game is afoot. Not a word. Into your clothes and come..." ABBE

"...I have no doubt that there were times when my life hung in the balance...." WIST

Sherlock Holmes Passes Go

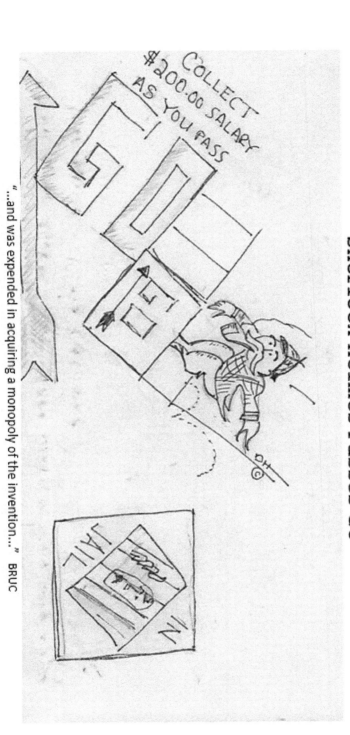

"...and was expended in acquiring a monopoly of the invention..."   BRUC

Sherlock Holmes: The Most Interesting Man in the World

"...I assure you that your little problem promises to be the most interesting which has come my way for some months..." COPP

Sherlock Holmes Visits Cabo San Lucus

" ...and they looked down upon the two broad sweep of beach at the foot of the great chalk cliff... "   LAST

Sherlock Holmes Goes Surfing

"...and sent two rolling waves to right and left of us..." SIGN

Sherlock Holmes Hitch-Hiking

"...Posted today in Gravesend by a man with a dirty thumb..." TWIS

Sherlock Holmes Goes Street Luging

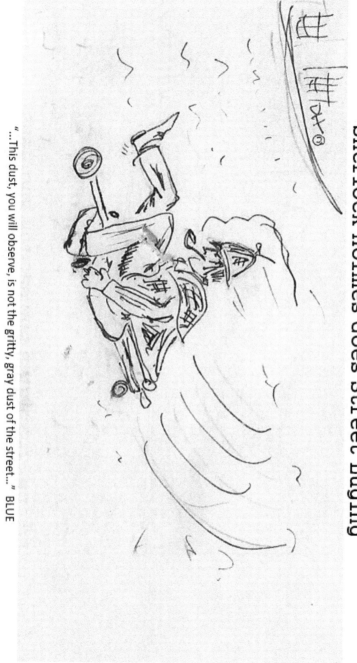

"...This dust, you will observe, is not the gritty, gray dust of the street..." BLUE

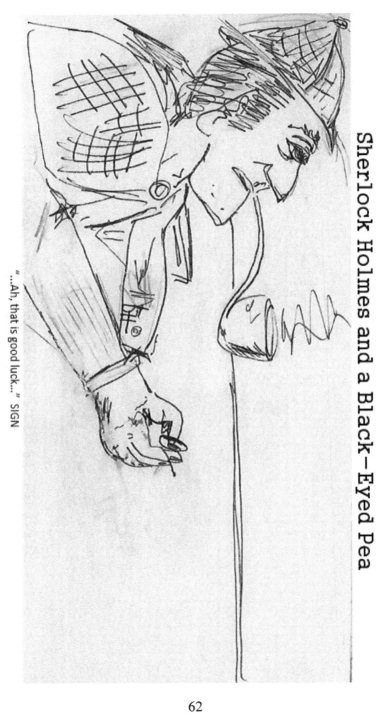

Sherlock Holmes and a Black–Eyed Pea

"...Ah, that is good luck..." SIGN

Sherlock Holmes Plays Marbles

"...with a smiling face and heart of marble, he will squeeze and squeeze and squeeze until he has drained them dry..." CHAS

Sherlock Holmes Disguised as a Tea Pot

" ...or he might adopt an elaborate disguise during the short time that he need be in London...." HOUN

Sherlock Holmes Practices Ballet

" ...Following the path backwards, we picked out another spot..." PRIO

Sherlock Holmes Goes for Donuts

" ...At breakfast he was sharp and fierce in manner, and made no allusion to the adventure of the night... " CREE

Sherlock Holmes Goes Shopping

"...The fact that he is doing his own shopping looks as though it were his wife..." GREE

"...at a touch from the Baron's chauffer, the car shivered and chuckled..." LAST

Sherlock Holmes Bird's Eye View.

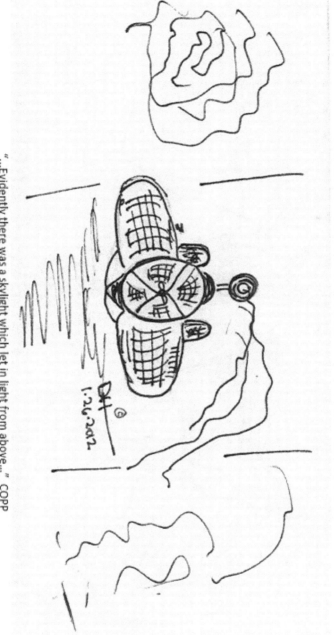

"...Evidently there was a skylight which let in light from above..." COPP

Sherlock Holmes Jumps Rope

"...He sank down into a crouching position and moved along upon his hands and feet, skipping every now and then as if he were overflowing with energy and vitality..." CREE

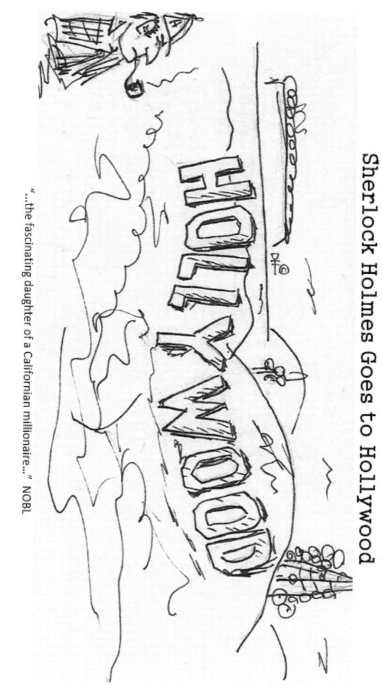

" ...the fascinating daughter of a Californian millionaire..." NOBL

Sherlock Holmes Roasts a Marshmallow

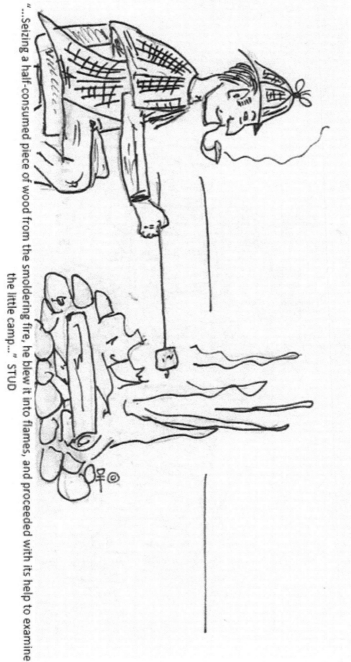

"...Seizing a half-consumed piece of wood from the smoldering fire, he blew it into flames, and proceeded with its help to examine the little camp..." STUD

Sherlock Holmes Repairs a Traffic Light

"...It was one of the main arteries which conveys the traffic of the city to the north and west..." REDH

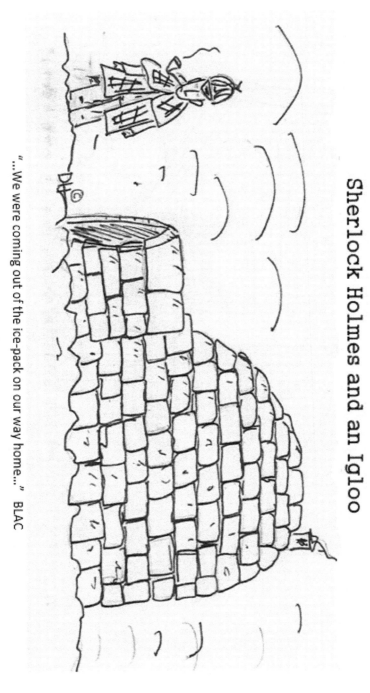

"...We were coming out of the ice-pack on our way home..."   BLAC

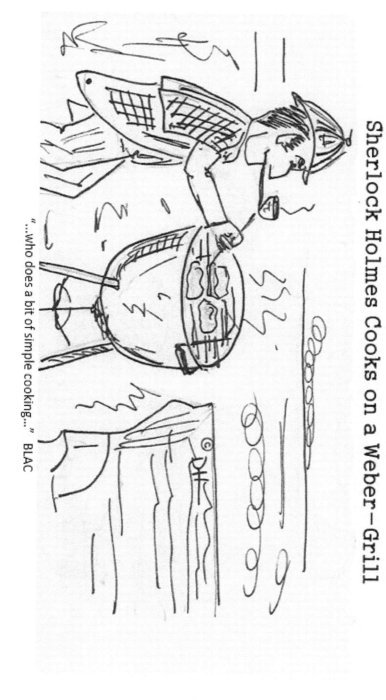

Sherlock Holmes Cooks on a Weber–Grill

"...who does a bit of simple cooking..." BLAC

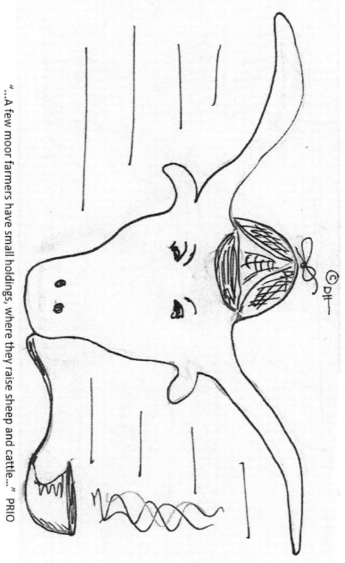

"...A few moor farmers have small holdings, where they raise sheep and cattle..." PRIO

"...he continued out loud, 'you will get food and drink...'" GLOR

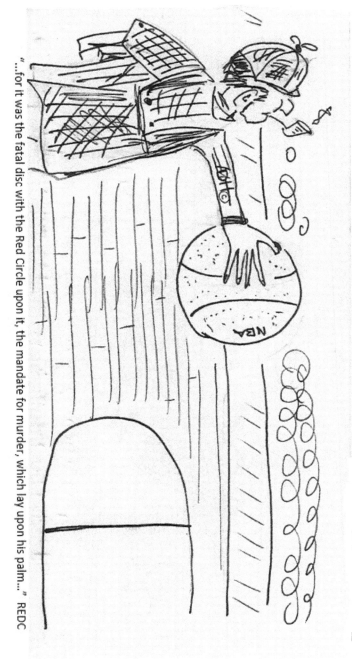

Sherlock Holmes Palms a Basketball

" ...for it was the fatal disc with the Red Circle upon it, the mandate for murder, which lay upon his palm..." REDC

"...What do you make of this string, Lestrade?..." CARD

Sherlock Holmes Does the Limbo

"...He was a fine figure of a man, tall, lithe, and agile, with a springy step and a pleasant, open face..." CARD

Sherlock Holmes Visits the Alamo

"...I was well aware that you could not do this without thinking of the mission..." CARD

"...But surely," I said, "the vampire was not necessarily a dead man?..." SUSS

Sherlock Holmes Plays Hockey

"...and I detected a mixture of mingled uneasiness and expectation beneath that mask which he was wont to assume..."   SIXN

83

Sherlock Holmes and an Air-Stream

"...But what a caravan..." STUD

Sherlock Holmes in Venice

"...These are from Italy...." 3GAB

Sherlock Holmes Does the Long Jump

"...Great Scott! Jump, Archie, jump and I'll swing for it..." REDH

Sherlock Holmes on a Flying Trapeze

"...I have every hope of reaching some conclusion..." DEVI

Sherlock Holmes Whacks a Pinata

"...Smack! Smack! Smack!..." COPP

Sherlock Holmes with a Banjo on His Knee

"...which was thrown across his knee..." NOBL

"...I was placed, however, in a comfortable boarding establishment at Edinburgh...." SIGN

"...We are, as usual, the irregulars, and we must take our own line of action...." LADY

91

Sherlock Holmes Disguised as a Mime

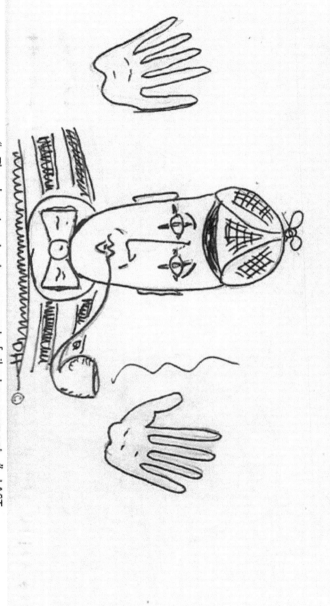

"...Then he sat gazing in a moment of silent amazement..." LAST

Sherlock Holmes Goes Fly Fishing

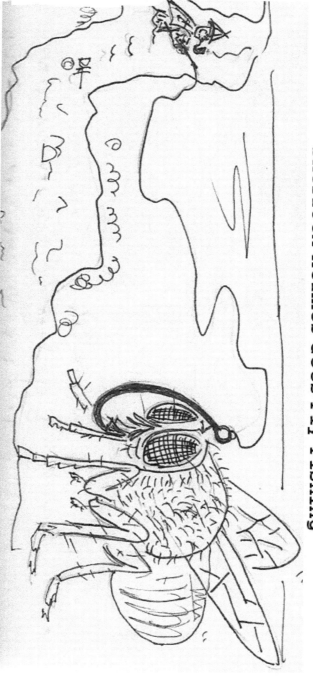

"...Is there good fishing in that part of Berkshire? The honest trainer showed very clearly upon his face that he was convinced that yet another lunatic had come into his harassed life...." SHOS

Sherlock Holmes Flies an Airplane

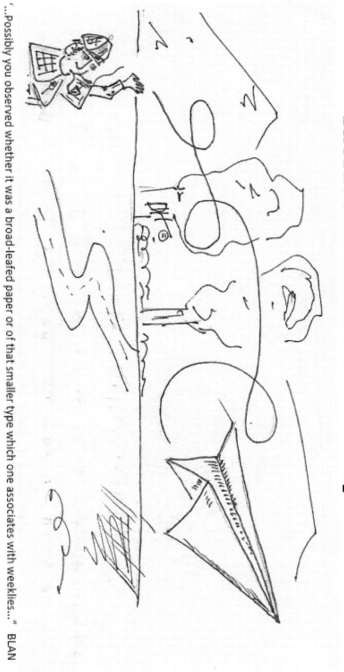

'...Possibly you observed whether it was a broad-leafed paper or of that smaller type which one associates with weeklies...' BLAN

94

Sherlock Holmes Gets Distorted

"...His drawn and distorted face told how terrible that agony had been..." LION

Sherlock Holmes buys NBC

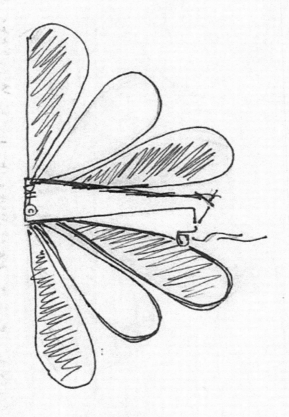

"...I found him strutting about as proud as a peacock..." SIGN

Sherlock Holmes Charms a Snake

"...and many a charming evening we have spent together..." HOUN

Sherlock Holmes Pumps Iron

"...He put less weight upon it. Why?..."   BOSC

98

Sherlock Holmes Visits the Hotel Del Coronado

" ...We were, I May say, seated in the old sitting room of the ancient hotel..." CREE

99

Sherlock Holmes Does Windows

"...Three small projections above the upper windows made a feeble attempt to justify its name...." 3GAB

Sherlock Holmes Steps into Quicksand

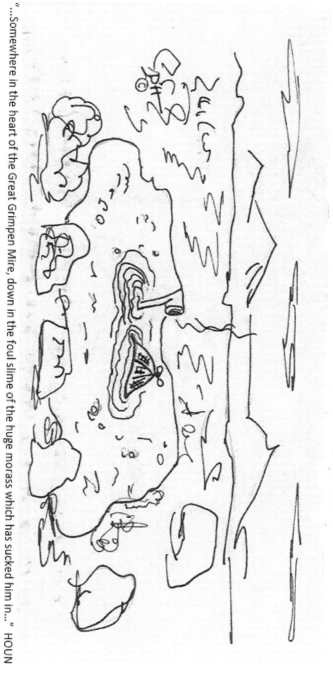

"...Somewhere in the heart of the Great Grimpen Mire, down in the foul slime of the huge morass which has sucked him in...." HOUN

Sherlock Holmes Watches a Toronado

"...As evening drew in, the storm grew higher and louder, and the wind cried and sobbed like a child in the chimney...."   FIVE

Sherlock Holmes Sitting in a Bird's Nest

"...Our birds are flown and the nest is empty," said Holmes..." GREE

"...You have done a great deal of digging, by your callosities...."   GLOR

Sherlock Holmes Works as a Life-Guard

"...He goes on to tell his own encounter with one when swimming off the coast of Kent..." LION

105

Sherlock Holmes Fires a Bazooka

"...I am not easily altered," said the old soldier...." BLAN

106

Sherlock Holmes Flies a Kite

"...flagons and trenchers flying before him..." HOUN

Sherlock Holmes Puts Out a Fire

"...fom which the spray rolls uplike the smoke from a burning house..." FINA

108

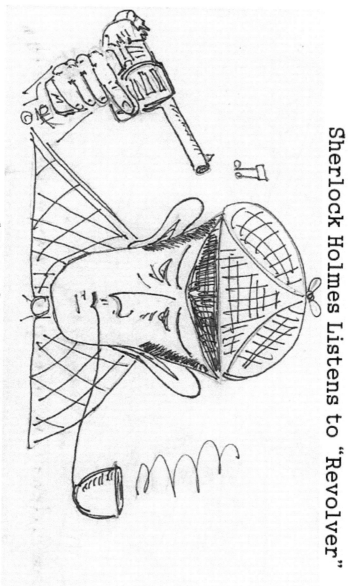

Sherlock Holmes Listens to "Revolver"

"...It is no use fingering your revolver...." MAZA

109

Sherlock Holmes Visits New Orleans

"...Then there was Mason of Bradford, and the notorious Muller, and Lefevre of Montpellier, and Samson of New Orleans..." STUD

Sherlock Holmes Throws a Javelin

"...Among other things, he had a long bamboo spear..." SIGN

Sherlock Holmes on a Trampoline

"...Brag and bounce," thought I to myself. "He knows that I cannot verify his guess...." STUD

Sherlock Holmes Coo—Coo—a—Choo

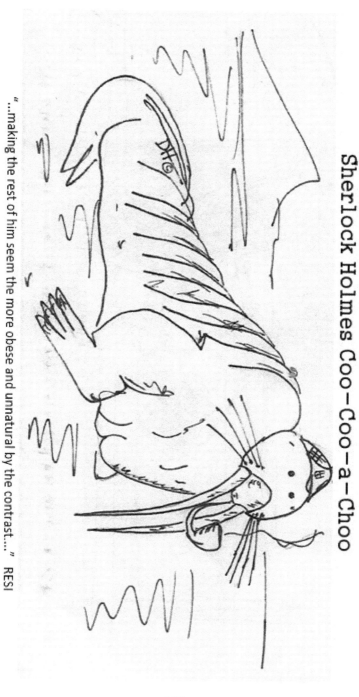

" ...making the rest of him seem the more obese and unnatural by the contrast...." RESI

"...It was a strange puzzle, and yet I knew that my mind could never know ease again until I had solved it...."   YELL

"...No; we don't keep a cat. But there is a cheetah and a baboon...." SPEC

Sherlock Holmes Visits the Colosseum

"...I realized it as I drove back and noted how hill after hill showed traces of ancient people...." HOUN

116

Sherlock Holmes Pins the Tail on a Donkey

"...Add to that the length of neck and head, and you get a creature not much less than two feet long -- probably more if there is any tail...." YELL

Sherlock Holmes Rides a Snowmobile

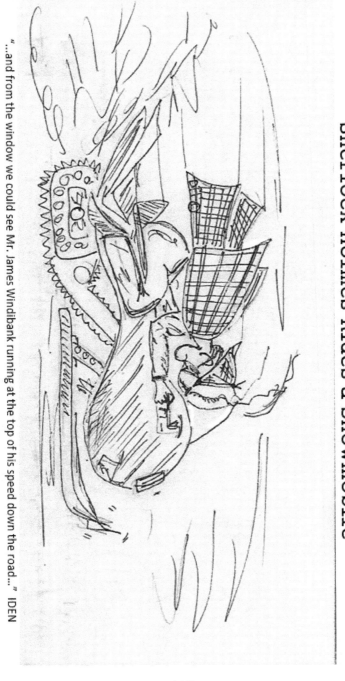

"...and from the window we could see Mr. James Windibank running at the top of his speed down the road..." IDEN

"...When you pass Bradley's, would you ask him to send up a pound of his strongest shag?..." HOUN

Sherlock Holmes Disguised as a Wal-Mart Greeter

WAL★MART

DHG
2.22.12

"...Ferrier ran to the door to greet the Mormon chief..." STUD

Sherlock Holmes Tosses a Pizza

"...I fancy the ashes of them might even now be found in that oven which already consumed a part...." SHOS

Sherlock Holmes Doubles In

"...These little darts, too, could only be shot in one way...." SIGN

DHC©
2.23.12

Sherlock Holmes Goes Curling

"...Already the first thin wisps of it were curling across the golden squares of the lighted window...." HOUN

Sherlock Holmes Visits the Parthenon

"...but he had not been in Greece..." GREE

"...His increasing fame had brought with it an immense practice..." BLAC

Sherlock Holmes Plays Dodgeball

"...I thought the police never could see through our dodge..." ABBE

Sherlock Holmes Had One Too Many

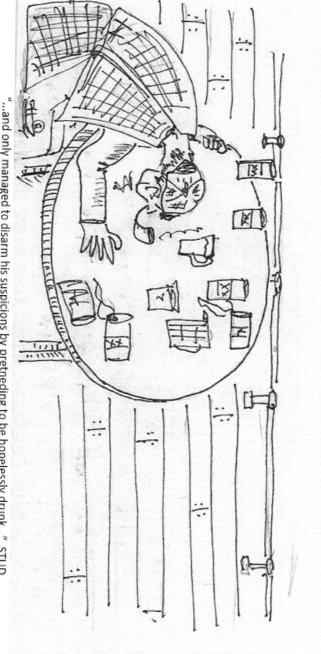

"...and only managed to disarm his suspicions by pretneding to be hopelessly drunk...." STUD

Sherlock Holmes Visits Germany in a V.W.

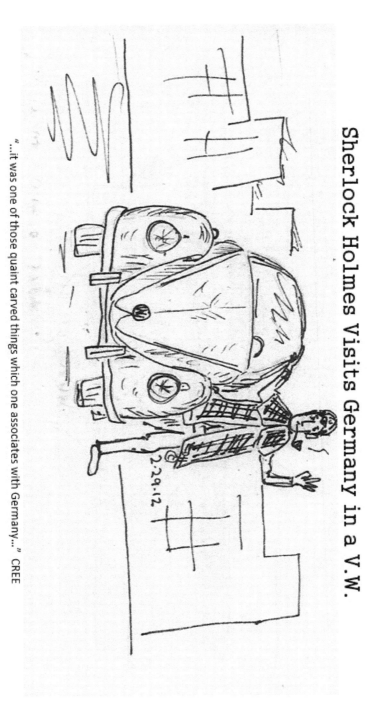

"...it was one of those quaint carved things which one associates with Germany..." CREE

Sherlock Holmes Visits the Serengeti.

"...It is used as an ordeal poison by the medicine-men in certain districts of West Africa..." DEVI

Sherlock Holmes Visits Oz

"...Holmes, you are a wizard..." RETI

Sherlock Holmes Enjoys Sushi

" ...He would eat raw meat and dance his war dance..." SIGN

"...and our friend, Armstrong, would have to drive through the Cam before he would shake Pompey off his trail..." MISS

Sherlock Holmes Picking Coffee Beans

"...He chuckled as he poured out the coffee..."   BLAC

Sherlock Holmes Does Stand-Up Comedy

"...Yet there was certainly an element of comedy..." 3GAR

"...This is: indeed like the old days..." EMPT

Sherlock Holmes Unwinds

"...And yet he would always wind up..." COPP

Sherlock Holmes Hangs a Shower Curtain

"...Through the gauze curtain our eyes were all rivited upon the scene within..." BLAC

Sherlock Holmes Tosses a Frisbie Over a Cliff

"...Just toss it over to me...." Card

"...I am extremely lazy...." STUD

"...The old colourman had the strength of a lion in that great trunk of his..." RETI

Sherlock Holmes Goes Wind Surfing

" ...I suddenly felt the wind blow upon my face..." ABBE

Sherlock Holmes Gets Bugged

"...And can you wonder that when I found this Crazy-boob of a bug-hunter with the queer name sitting right on top of it..." 3GAR

Sherlock Holmes Cheers for His Team

"...What is the the root of it ..." REDC

143

Sherlock Holmes Embraces Cloud Technology

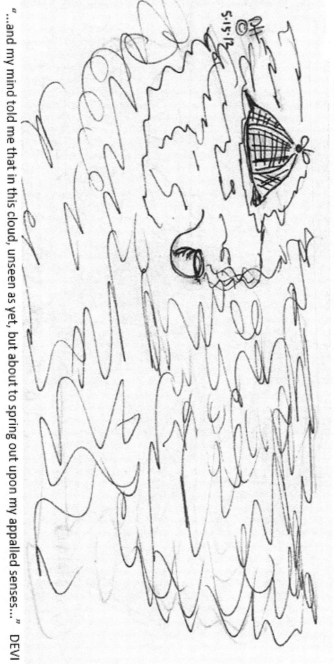

"...and my mind told me that in this cloud, unseen as yet, but about to spring out upon my appalled senses..." DEVI

Sherlock Holmes Rides a Penny-Farthing

"...You shall not have a farthing from me..." BERY

DH
3.30.12

Sherlock Holmes Visits Newburg, NY

"...When we have him by the heels we can see if New York can't help us keep him...." REDC

146

"...You did not tell me that you intended to go into harness...." SCAN

Sherlock Holmes Swims with the Dolphins

"...Summer and winter he went for his swim, and as I am a swimmer myself, I have often joined him..." LION

"...putting out a broad, flat hand, like the flipper of a seal..."   BLAC

Sherlock Holmes Enjoys Halloween, Again

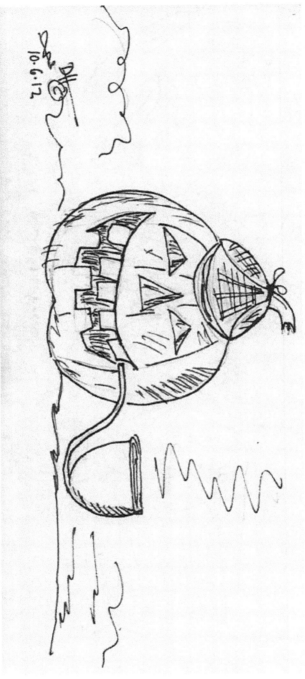

10.6.12

"...Then it was turn, and I went through him as if he had been a rotten pumpkin...." ABBE

Sherlock Holmes: Jedi Master

"...I understand now, what should never have forgotten, that I am the pupil and you are the master..." BLAC

Sherlock Holmes Visits Yucatan

"...It's more than a precious stone. It's *the* precious stone..."   BLUE

Sherlock Holmes Enjoys Chianti in Venice

"...May I offer you a glass of Chianti, Miss Morston?..." CARD

Sherlock Holmes Investigates Big Foot

"...But Holmes had jammed it with his foot..." LADY

Sherlock Holmes Enjoys Tarzan

"...He was more like a malignant and cunning ape than a human being..."   EMPY

"...Perhaps not with your tongue, my dear Watson, but certainly with your eyebrows..." CARD

Sherlock Holmes in a Hammock

" …in the out stretched palm…." FIVE

157

Sherlock Holmes Visits Sydney

"...The bridge, no doubt, was too crowded, even on such a night, for their purpose..." FIVE

Sherlock Holmes Visits Mt. Fuji

"...you have visited Japan ..." GLOR

Sherlock Holmes Hails a Tram

" ...It is as if you met a tram-car coming down a country lane...." BRUC

"...I have endeavoured to give some account of my strange experiences..." FINA

"...I don't know if any of you gentlemen have ever read or heard anything of that old fort...." FIVE

162

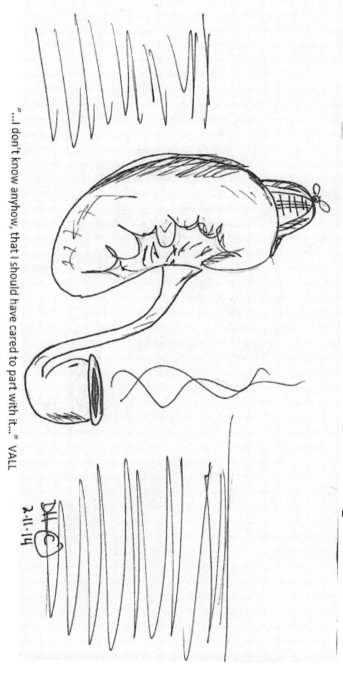

"...I don't know anyhow, that I should have cared to part with it..." VALL

"...It looked like a great shimmering ice-field..." HOUN

Sherlock Holmes Enjoys the Garden

"...I must explore the garden and see what I could find...." BLAN

DHG
2·16·14

Sherlock Holmes Visits Madrid

"...murdered in their rooms at the Hotel Escurial at Madrid..." WIST

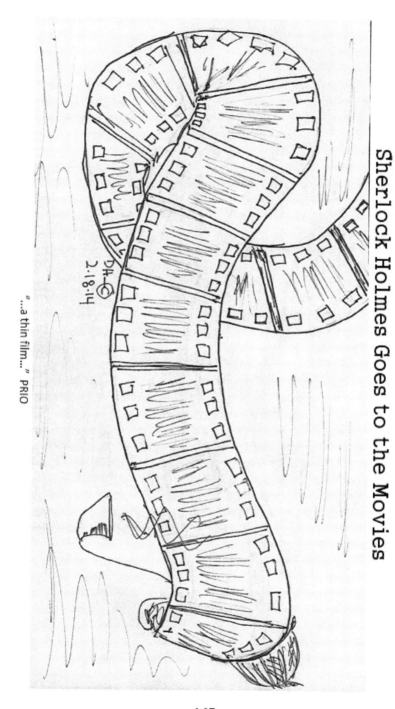

"...a thin film...." PRIO

Sherlock Holmes Visits Florida

"...My uncle Elias emigraed to America, when he was a young man and became a planter in Florida..." FIVE

Sherlock Holmes Mushroom

"...so that a crop of livid fungi was growing on the side of it..." MUSG

DH
2-2014

Sherlock Holmes Chainsaw Massacre

"...and I SAW what he held in his hand..."   EMPT

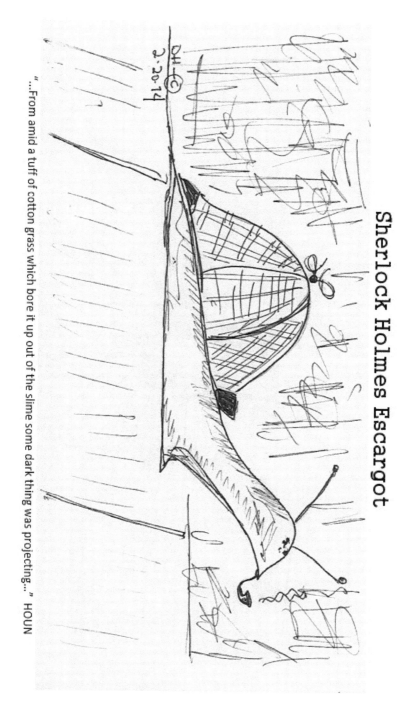

Sherlock Holmes Escargot

"...From amid a tuff of cotton grass which bore it up out of the slime some dark thing was projecting..." HOUN

171

Sherlock Holmes Got Milk?

"...if I might have a glass of milk and a biscuit..." PRIO

Sherlock Holmes Visits Japan

"...the Japanese system of wrestling..." EMPT

Sherlock Holmes at Delicate Arch, UT

"...the broad valley of Utah bathed in sunlight..." STUD

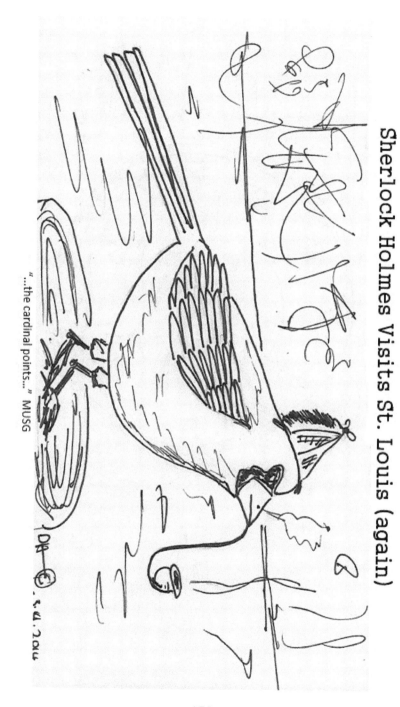

"...the cardinal points..." MUSG

Sherlock Holmes Visits St. Louis (again)

"...For an hour or more he was at work..." BERY

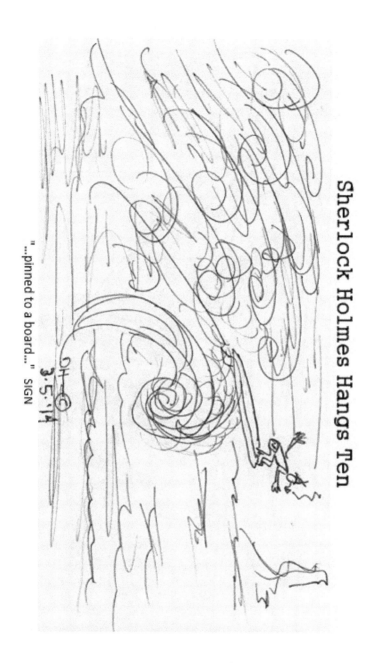

Sherlock Holmes Hangs Ten

"...pinned to a board..." SIGN

Sherlock Holmes is the Master's Voice

"...said he in a crackling voice..." BLUE

VICTOR

DH—C
2.6.'96

Sherlock Holmes Loves Canada

"...and in Canada..." HOUN

179

Sherlock Holmes at the Iditerod

"...still deep in snow...." FINA

DH© 3·10·'14

180

Sherlock Holmes Outstanding in His Field

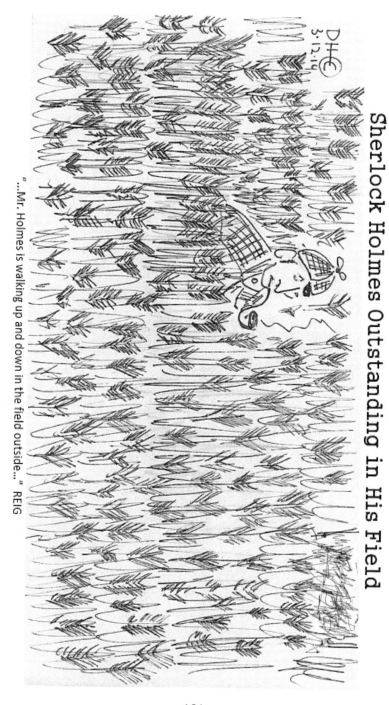

"...Mr. Holmes is walking up and down in the field outside..." REIG

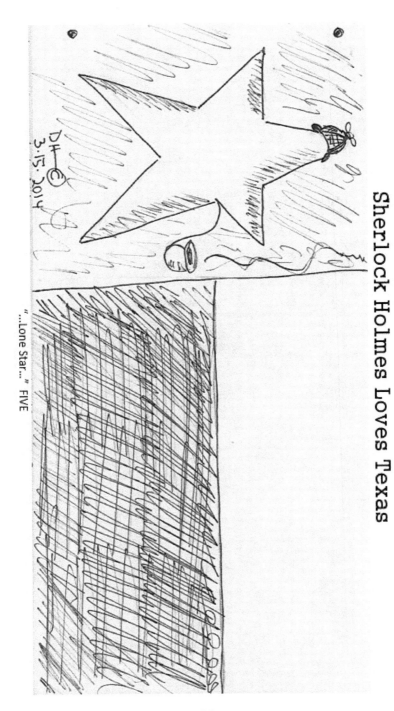

"...Lone Star..." FIVE

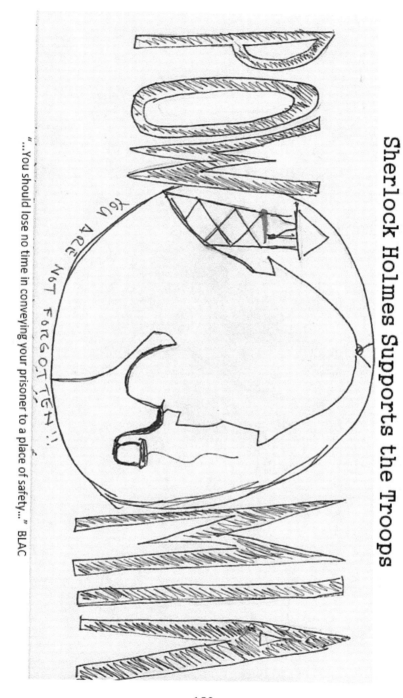

Sherlock Holmes Supports the Troops

"...You should lose no time in conveying your prisoner to a place of safety..." BLAC

YOU ARE NOT FORGOTTEN!!

Sherlock Holmes Predicts the Future

"...We shall understand each other better in the future..." LION

3-18-94

Sherlock Holmes Visits the French Quarter

"...driven away no doubt by the foul reek of the surrounding swamp...." HOUN

"...i dare say you thought I acted rather badly to Stanley Hopkins just now...." ABBE

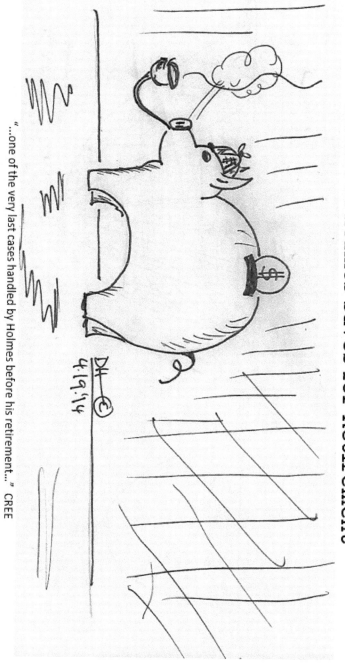

Sherlock Holmes Saves for Retirement

"...one of the very last cases handled by Holmes before his retirement..." CREE

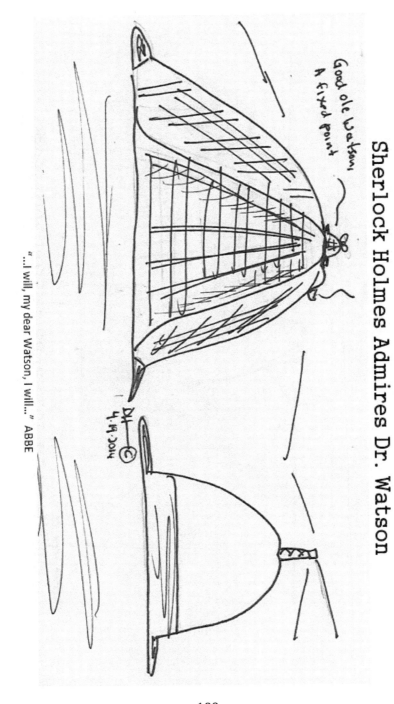

Sherlock Holmes Admires Dr. Watson

Good ole Watson,
A fixed point

" ...I will, my dear Watson, I will..." ABBE

188

Sherlock Holmes Goes to the Dentist

" ...they should have the same tooth...." STOC

Sherlock Holmes Tests the Water with His Toe

"...This is the proof that he feels my toe..." MAZA

Sherlock Holmes Positions His
Hands at 10 & 2 on the Steering Wheel

"...More wise than those who go on until the wheel turns against them..." HOUN

"...Give me your coat and umbrella," said Holmes...." FIVE

"...with the results of driving it through the ventilator..." SPEC

Sherlock Holmes Strolls in Zurich

"...when we were in Switzerland..." EMPT

Sherlock Holmes Visits Rio

" ...a missionary from South America... " LADY

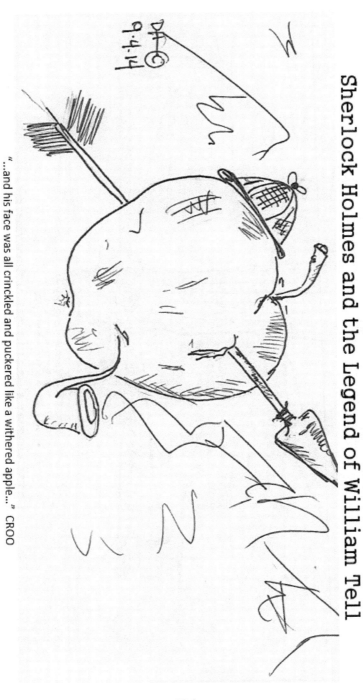

"...and his face was all crinckled and puckered like a withered apple..." CROO

196

Sherlock Holmes Visits the Mexico Pyramids

"...On the palm were three little pyramids of dark doughy clay...." 3STU

DH©
9.16.2014

197

Sherlock Holmes Does Downward Dog

"...Then stretching himself upon his face and leaning his chin upon his hands..." SILV

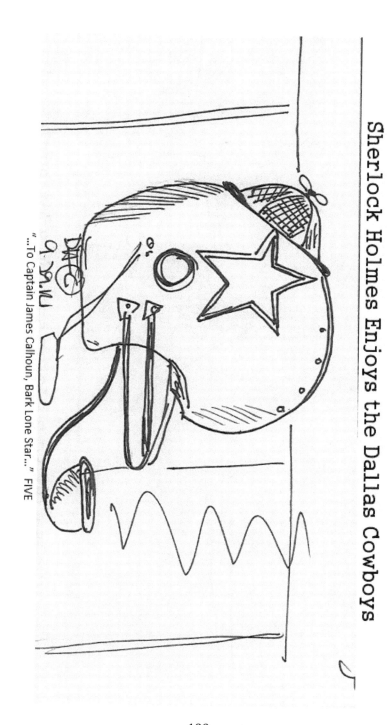

" ...To Captain James Calhoun, Bark Lone Star...." FIVE

199

Sherlock Holmes Enjoys a Large Martini

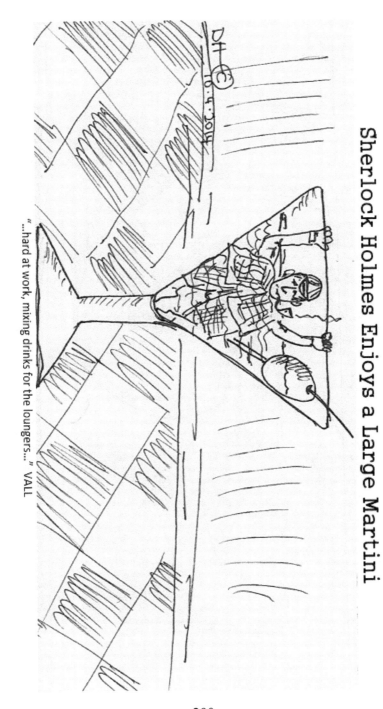

"...hard at work, mixing drinks for the loungers..." VALL

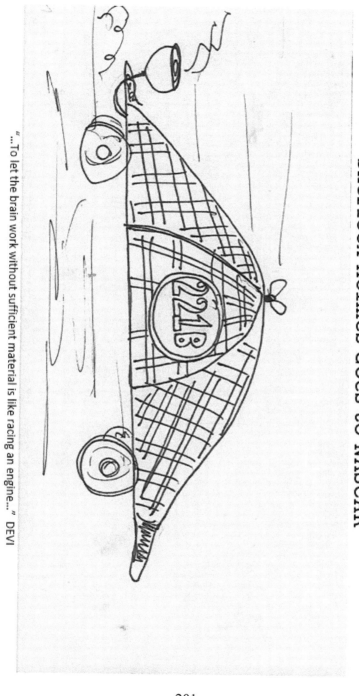

"...To let the brain work without sufficient material is like racing an engine..."   DEVI

Sherlock Holmes Visits the Duomo

"...I found myself in Florence..." EMPT

202

Sherlock Holmes Visits Pisa

"...Well, there is the tower of the cathedral..." COPP

DH
10-22-14

"...These two people are presumably dead, or we should have heard their story before now..." CARD

204

Sherlock Holmes Visits Downton Abbey

"...I had intended "The Adventures of the Abbey Grange" to be the last of these exploits of my friend Mr. Sherlock Holmes...." SECO

Sherlock Holmes Disguised as Sock Monkey

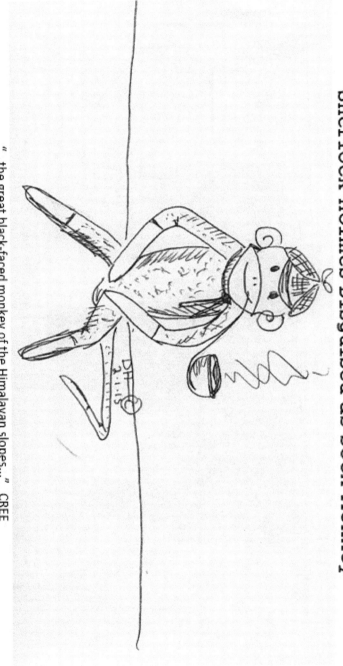

"...the great black-faced monkey of the Himalayan slopes..." CREE

Sherlock Holmes Visits Puxsutawny Phil

"...I could see a shawdow pass over his face...." COPP

"...Then I will help you with all my heart..." DANC

Sherlock Holmes Uses a Glock

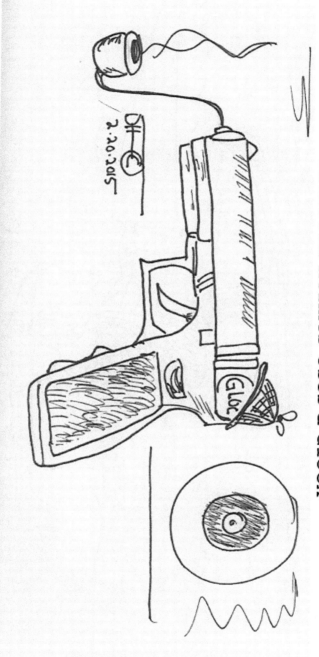

"...Pull up, man!" he yelled, drawing a pistol from his side...." SOLI

"...That's why I gave you water..." DYIN

210

Sherlock Holmes on a Rocking Horse

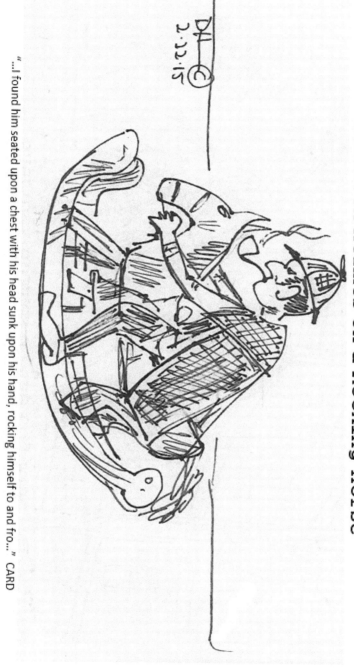

"...I found him seated upon a chest with his head sunk upon his hand, rocking himself to and fro..." CARD

Sherlock Holmes on the Log Ride

"...built himself a substantial log-house..." STUD

Sherlock Holmes Has a Mole Removed

"...A mole could trace it..." BOSC

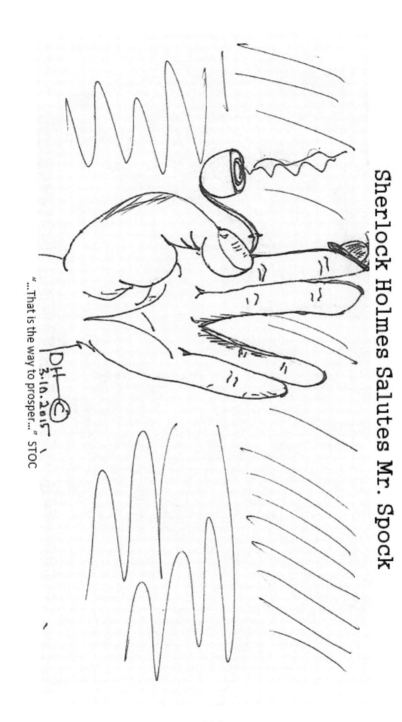

Sherlock Holmes Salutes Mr. Spock

"...That is the way to prosper..." SТОС

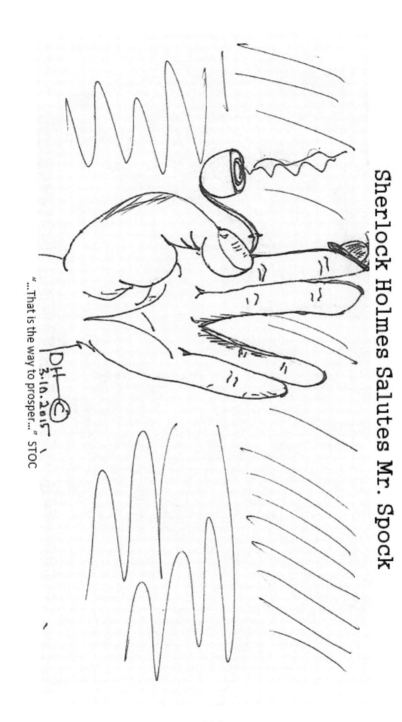

214

Sherlock Holmes Visits Mt. Etna

"...We cannot live forever on such a volcano..." SECO

Sherlock Holmes Enjoys a Cheeseburger

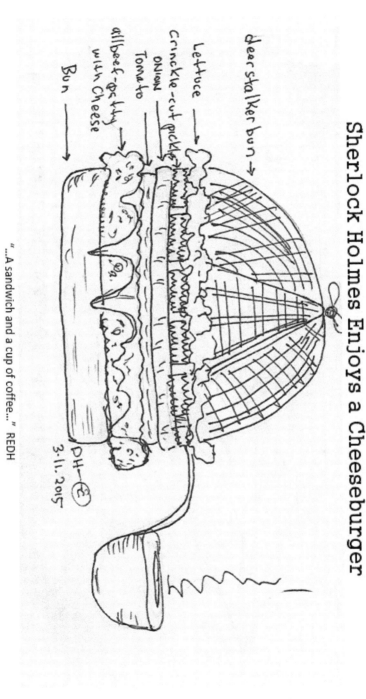

deerstalker bun →

Lettuce

Crinckle-cut pickle

Onion

Tomato

allbeef-patty
with Cheese

Bun

DH—Ⓔ
3-11.2015

"...A sandwich and a cup of coffee..." REDH

216

Sherlock Holmes Waiting at the Catania Airport

"...who knocked out my left canine in the waiting room...." EMPT

DIVIETO di INGRESSO

DH
3·14·2015

Sherlock Holmes in His Ray–Ban Aviators

"...with gray-tinted sunglasses?..." RETI

DH
3·14·2015

Sherlock Holmes on Top of the World

"...And now on the top..." ABBE

Sherlock Holmes Loves Flying Frogs

"...this impassive and still dignified figure crouching froglike upon the ground..."   CREE

DH—©
3·17·2015

Sherlock Holmes Smoking Gnats?

"...then he lit his pipe and sat some time smoking and turning them over..." GLOR

DH
3·18·15

"...if you would have the goodness to put the Japanese vase to one side...."   3GAR

Sherlock Holmes Celebrates Easter 2015

"...with the intention of visiting the rabbit warren..." 3GAR

DH© 4·5·2015

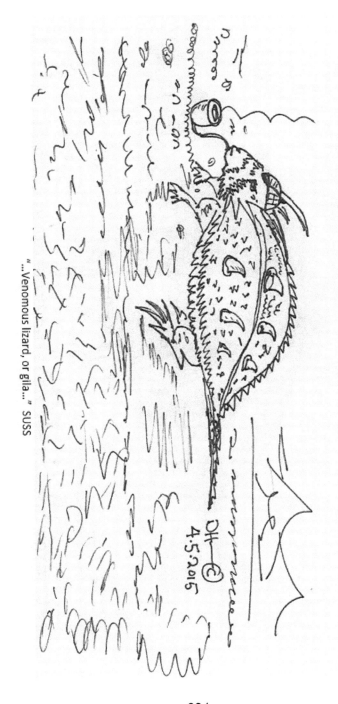

Sherlock Holmes Loves Horned-Toads

"...Venomous lizard, or gila..." SUSS

224

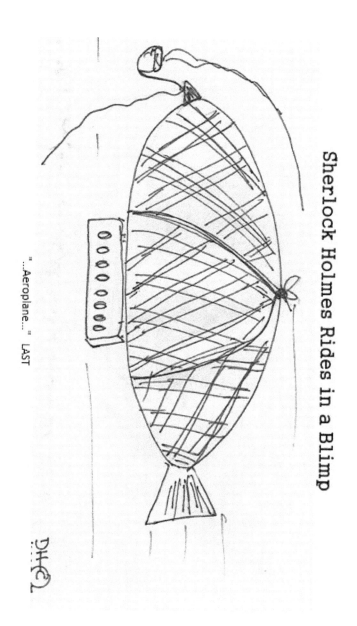

Sherlock Holmes Rides in a Blimp

"...Aeroplane..." LAST

Sherlock Holmes Tries Botox

"...Ryder passed his tongue over his parched lips...." BLUE

5·20·2015